MW00613266

Dorrie

and the Play

To Ann

EGMONT

We bring stories to life

First published in Great Britain as *Dorrie's Play* 1976.
This edition first published in Great Britain 2015 by Egmont UK Limited
The Yellow Building, 1 Nicholas Road, London W11 4AN
www.egmont.co.uk

ISBN 978 1 4052 8002 0

A CIP catalogue record for this title is available from the British Library.

Dorrie and the Play

by Patricia Coombs

EGMONT

This is Dorrie. She is a witch. A little witch. Her hat is always on crooked and her socks don't match, and wherever Dorrie goes her black cat Gink goes with her.

One Thursday, the day of the Fancy Dress Ball, Dorrie swept her room. She found a pair of socks that matched and hung them on her chair.

Dorrie skipped down the hall to her mother's room and Gink went with her.

The Big Witch was lying in bed with a towel over her head.

'Mother,' said Dorrie, 'I've come to sweep your room for you.'

The Big Witch opened one eye. 'NO! Thank you,' said the Big Witch. 'I have a headache, and I'm taking a nap. Why don't you take a nap, too?'

Dorrie skipped downstairs and Gink went with her. Dorrie went into the kitchen.

Cook was stirring batter in a big bowl with one hand and taking muffins out of the oven with the other.

'Cook,' said Dorrie, 'I've come to sweep the kitchen for you.'

'NO! Thank you,' said Cook, frowning and muttering and stirring faster and faster. 'I'm much too busy to be helped. Go and take a nap.'

Dorrie went out into the hall and Gink went with her.

'I don't want to take a nap,' said Dorrie. 'Whenever Cook or Mother is tired I have to take a nap.'

Dorrie tiptoed down the hall. She peeped into the parlour.

'Gink,' said Dorrie, 'let's put on a play. You'll be the Wicked Magician. You'll also be the Prince, and I'll be the Princess.'

Dorrie put the broom across two chairs.

'There,' said Dorrie. 'That will be the stage. Now we need some curtains.'

Dorrie skipped down the hall and into the sewing room. It was a mess. There were piles of cloth, and clothes to be mended, and patterns and buttons and spools of thread and pins and needles.

Dorrie picked up some cloth. 'This would make very nice curtains,' said Dorrie.

Dorrie took the cloth and a pair of scissors and went out into the kitchen.

Cook was muttering and banging pots and pans around.

'Cook,' said Dorrie.

'Oh, my goodness, I thought you were taking a nap,' said Cook crossly. 'What is it now?'

'I'm making a surprise for you and Mother, and I wanted you to cut this old piece of cloth for me right across here.'

'Oh, all right,' grumbled Cook. 'Give it to me, but then you run along and stay out of the kitchen.'

Cook cut the cloth.

'Oh, thank you, Cook,' said Dorrie. 'I won't bother you any more.'

Dorrie went back into the sewing room and filled her pockets with safety pins and skipped back into the parlour. Gink went with her.

Dorrie pinned the cloth around the broom handle. Gink stuck his head out between the curtains and looked at Dorrie.

'Come on, Gink,' said Dorrie. 'Now I will dress you up as a magician. You will be Gink the Great.'

Dorrie skipped back to the sewing room and Gink went with her.

Dorrie found a piece of cloth and pinned it around Gink for a cloak. She found one of her mittens in the mending basket and tried it on Gink.

It just fit, and it made a fine hat for a magician.

Dorrie found another piece of cloth that was just right for a princess. Dorrie pinned it round herself and looked in the mirror.

'I need a crown,' said Dorrie.

She skipped down the hall and into the kitchen and Gink went with her.

'Cook,' said Dorrie, 'I need something else.'

'Oh, my GOODNESS,' cried Cook, 'what is it now?'

'That round tin with the hole in it, may I try it on?'

'Oh, all right,' grumbled Cook.

Dorrie opened the cupboard. She tried on the cake tin. It was too small. She tried on the flan ring. It was just right.

Dorrie ran upstairs and got a box of gold stars from under her bed. She stuck them all over the crown.

'Come on, Gink,' said Dorrie, 'we've got to hurry. Mother is going to be getting ready for the Fancy Dress Ball and she won't have time to see the play.'

Dorrie took the crown and the pieces of cloth and put them in the parlour behind the curtains. She skipped into the dining room and got the dinner bell. Then she peeped into the kitchen. Cook was busy taking things out of the oven.

Dorrie tiptoed over to the refrigerator and opened the door very quietly.

'WHAT ARE YOU DOING IN THE REFRIGERATOR?' roared Cook. 'You'll spoil your appetite.'

'I'm not doing anything in the refrigerator,' said Dorrie. 'I just need a little something for the surprise. I'm not going to eat it.'

Dorrie slipped a tin of sardines into her pocket and closed the refrigerator.

'Cook,' said Dorrie, 'my surprise for you and Mother is almost ready. When I ring the dinner bell come into the parlour and sit down. I've been working very hard and you've just got to come.'

'Hmph,' said Cook. 'Well, all right, I'll come.'

Dorrie went upstairs and Gink went with her. She peeped into her mother's room. The Big Witch was sitting on the bed, frowning.

'Mother,' said Dorrie, 'do you still have a headache?'

The Big Witch looked gloomily at Dorrie. 'Miss Dorp is my headache. She always wins the prize for the best costume at the Ball. It makes my head ache when I think about it.'

'Oh,' said Dorrie. 'Well, I have been making a surprise for you. It will cheer you up. I've invited Cook, too. When I ring the dinner bell will you come into the parlour?'

The Big Witch frowned. 'Oh, all right,' she answered.

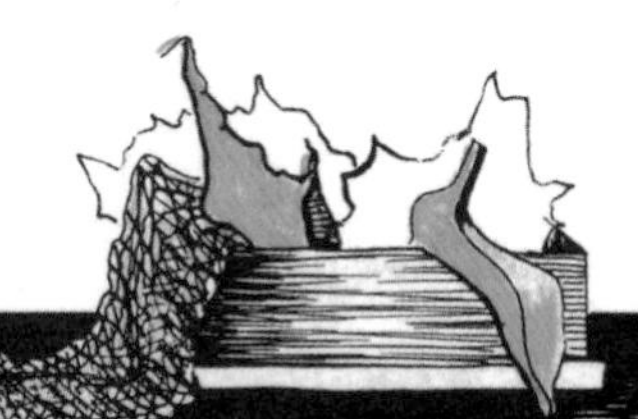

Dorrie ran downstairs and into the parlour and Gink went with her.

Dorrie pinned her robes round her and put on her crown. Then she dressed Gink in his cloak and hat.

Dorrie reached into her pocket and got something and put it in the middle of the stage. It was a sardine.

Gink ate it. He wanted more. He looked at Dorrie.

Dorrie shook her head. 'You'll have more sardines after a while, Gink. They will keep you on stage doing what you are supposed to do.'

Dorrie rang the dinner bell and peeped through the curtains. As soon as the Big Witch and Cook sat down, Dorrie pulled the curtains back and stood in the middle of the stage.

'Ladies and gentlemen,' said Dorrie. 'This play is called "The Princess and the Magician". I am the Princess and Gink is the Magician – Gink the Great.

‘The Princess is walking in the Royal Gardens. She is picking flowers. Gink the Great is following her, but the Princess does not know it. The poor Princess does not know that Gink the Great is about to be wicked and cast a spell over her.’

Dorrie walked back and forth and leaned down every few steps, pretending to pick flowers from the carpet. She had to be careful her crown did not fall off.

Gink smelled the sardines in Dorrie's pocket. Gink followed Dorrie back and forth, back and forth.

Gink stepped on his magician's cloak and stumbled. He got all tangled up.

Dorrie stopped picking flowers.

'Gink the Great has just cast a wicked spell over the poor Princess,' said Dorrie. 'It was such a bad spell he got tangled up in his cloak.'

Dorrie reached under her robes and got another sardine from her pocket. Gink got untangled and stood on his hind legs, waiting for the sardine.

'Gink the Great is looking to see if his wicked spell is going to work,' explained Dorrie. 'Now he is going to run away so nobody will know he did it.' And Dorrie tossed the sardine behind the curtains and Gink ran to get it.

‘That is the end of Act One,’ Dorrie said. Dorrie closed the curtains. She took the cloak and mitten off Gink.

Dorrie tucked a sardine into the rim of her crown. She opened the curtains again, closed her eyes, and stretched out on the carpet.

Dorrie opened one eye.

‘A hundred years have passed. A handsome prince, Prince Gink, is galloping through the forest to save the Princess. He’ll be here in a minute.’

Gink came out from behind the curtains. He sniffed and came closer and closer to Dorrie. He sniffed Dorrie’s hand. Then he sniffed the crown. He knocked the crown off and ate the sardine.

Dorrie stood up. She made a curtsy.

'Thank you, Prince Gink. You have saved me from the spell of the wicked Magician. Now we can live happily ever after.'

Dorrie went behind the curtains. The Big Witch and Cook clapped and clapped.

The Big Witch was smiling. 'That was a lovely play, Dorrie,' said the Big Witch. 'I feel much better.'

'How did you get Gink to go back and forth like that?' asked Cook.

Dorrie looked up at Cook and smiled. 'Sardines,' said Dorrie. 'That was the secret in the refrigerator.'

'Oh,' said Cook. 'Maybe you had better have your bath before supper.'

Dorrie took her bath and Gink sat on the window sill and licked his paws and washed his face.

Dorrie put on a clean dress and went downstairs to the kitchen and Gink went with her.

Dorrie was just finishing her supper, and Cook was washing the dishes when the kitchen door opened suddenly.

It was the Big Witch.

Cook dropped a kettle.

'Oh, my,' said Dorrie in a small voice.

'WHAT HAPPENED TO MY COSTUME?' said the Big Witch. 'Look at it, just look!'

'Oh, my,' said Dorrie.

'OH, NO!' wailed Cook. 'Oh, why didn't I look at the cloth before I cut it!'

'I'm sorry, Mother,' said Dorrie. 'It just looked like a funny old dress.'

The Big Witch and Cook and Dorrie thought and thought.

Dorrie looked at her mother.

'Mother,' said Dorrie, 'you could go to the Fancy Dress Ball as a little witch.'

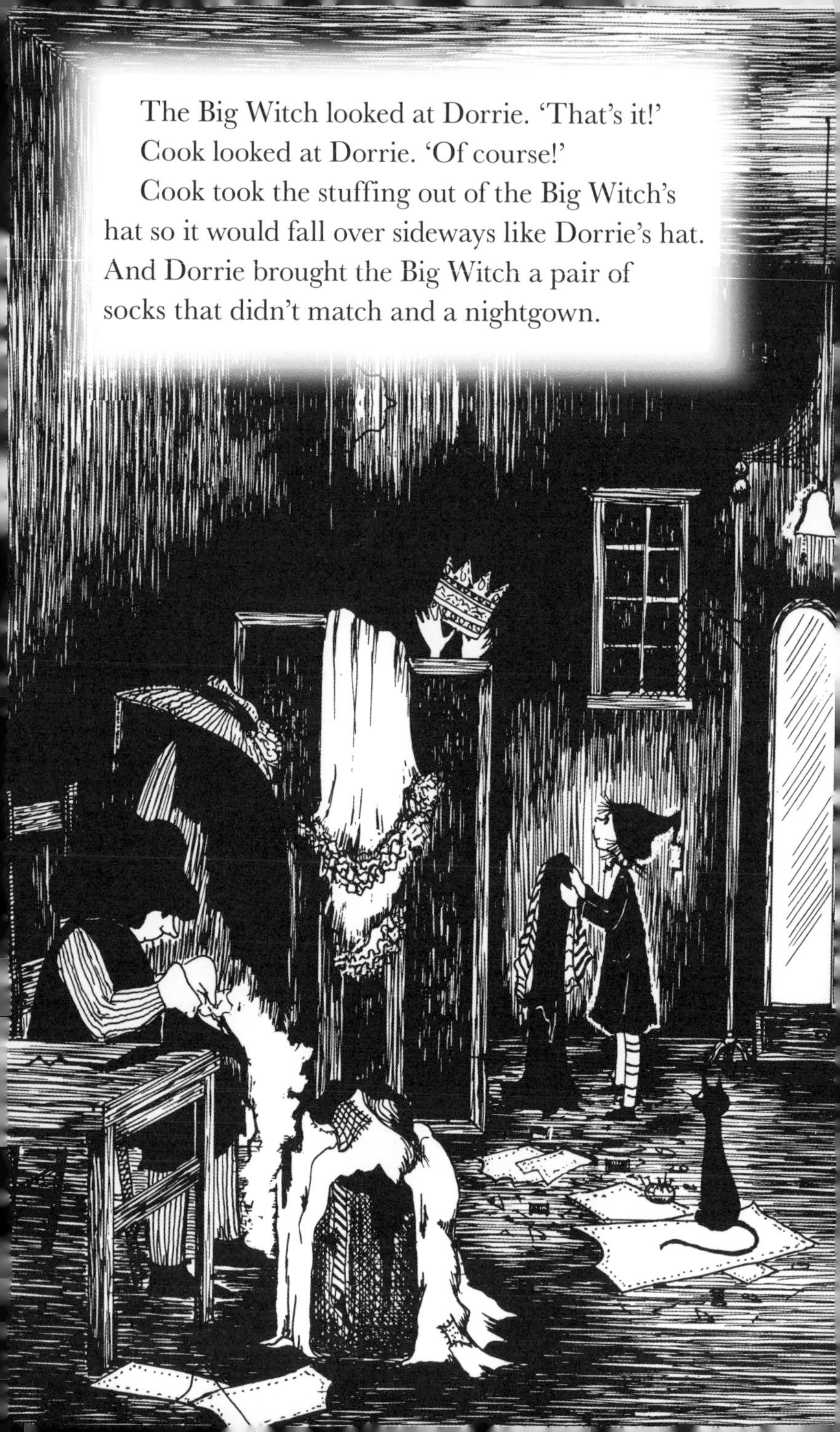

The Big Witch looked at Dorrie. 'That's it!'

Cook looked at Dorrie. 'Of course!'

Cook took the stuffing out of the Big Witch's hat so it would fall over sideways like Dorrie's hat. And Dorrie brought the Big Witch a pair of socks that didn't match and a nightgown.

The doorbell rang.

'I'm almost ready,' said the Big Witch. 'Tell everyone I'll be right there.'

Dorrie opened the door.

'Oh, my,' said Dorrie, 'you all look wonderful. Mother will be along in a minute.'

Mr Obs was dressed as a pincushion.

Squig was dressed as an umbrella.

Dinger was dressed as an ice-cream cone.

Miss Dorp was dressed as a queen.

'Why, I thought you were going to dress as a queen, too!' cried Miss Dorp.

The Big Witch smiled. 'I changed my mind. It was changed by mistake, but I like this better.'

'It is the best costume I have ever seen,' said Mr Obs. 'I like elves.'

'I like elves better than pincushions,' said Squig.
'I like elves better than umbrellas,' said Dinger.
'*I* like QUEENS, with lots of ruffles and beads and lace,' said Miss Dorp crossly.

And with that, they all called 'good night' to Dorrie and Cook and went off to the Ball.

Dorrie and Cook waved to them from the doorway.

'Well,' said Cook, 'your play had a happy ending after all, even if people can't tell the difference between a little witch and an elf.'

'I suppose it's hard to tell sometimes,' said Dorrie. 'And I'm sorry I bothered you when you were busy.'

Cook smiled. 'I am always busy. Sometimes I am busy being busy. And now it's time for you to go to bed.'

Dorrie climbed up the stairs and Gink went with her.
In a few minutes she was sound asleep under the covers. Gink curled up on her socks on the floor beside the bed.

The clock in the hall struck midnight.

The Big Witch came home, and tiptoed up the stairs to Dorrie's room.

e Big Witch was smiling.

rrie sat up.

ı, Mother,' said Dorrie, 'did you win?'

e Big Witch laughed. 'Mr Obs and I both won.

r Obs' pins fell out and he won first prize as a

o, and I won first prize as an elf.'

n glad,' said Dorrie.

e too,' said the Big Witch.

Dorrie fell asleep again with a big smile on her face.

And so did the Big Witch.

And so did Mr Obs.